P9-CDI-011

DISCARD

Cats for sale!

"**W**hat's a catalog?" Huey asked me.

"A catalog," I said, "is where cats come from. You open the catalog, and the cats jump out. Then they run outside and work in the garden."

"I don't believe you," Huey said. "Cats don't act like that."

"Of course," I said, "*ordinary* cats don't act like that. That's why you have to get them specially—catalog cats."

"Really?" Huey said.

"Really," I said.

by Ann Cameron

JULIAN'S WORLD

THE STORIES JULIAN TELLS

by Ann Cameron

illustrated by Ann Strugnell

A STEPPING STONE BOOK™

Random House 🏠 New York

Sale of this book without a front cover may be unauthorized. If the book is coverless, it may have been reported to the publisher as "unsold or destroyed" and neither the author nor the publisher may have received payment for it.

This is a work of fiction. Names, characters, places, and incidents either are the product of the author's imagination or are used fictitiously. Any resemblance to actual persons, living or dead, events, or locales is entirely coincidental.

Text copyright © 1981 by Ann Cameron
Interior illustrations copyright © 1981 by Ann Strugnell
Cover illustration copyright © by Robert Papp

All rights reserved. Published in the United States by Random House Children's Books, a division of Penguin Random House LLC, New York. Originally published in hardcover by Pantheon Books, an imprint of Random House Children's Books, a division of Penguin Random House LLC, New York, in 1981.

Random House and the colophon are registered trademarks and A Stepping Stone Book and the colophon are trademarks of Penguin Random House LLC.

Visit us on the Web!
rhcbooks.com

Educators and librarians, for a variety of teaching tools,
visit us at RHTeachersLibrarians.com

Library of Congress Cataloging-in-Publication Data is available upon request.
ISBN 978-0-394-82892-3 (trade) — ISBN 978-0-525-57981-6 (lib. bdg.) —
ISBN 978-0-307-80119-7 (ebook)

Printed in the United States of America
10 9 8 7 6 5 4 3 2 1

This book has been officially leveled by using the F&P Text Level Gradient™ Leveling System.

Random House Children's Books supports the First Amendment
and celebrates the right to read.

R0452297063

CONTENTS

The Pudding
Like a
Night on the Sea

"I'm going to make something special for your mother," my father said.

My mother was out shopping. My father was in the kitchen, looking at the pots and the pans and the jars of this and that.

"What are you going to make?" I said.

"A pudding," he said.

My father is a big man with wild black hair. When he laughs, the sun laughs in the window-panes. When he thinks, you can almost see his thoughts sitting on all the tables and chairs. When he is angry, me and my little brother, Huey, shiver to the bottom of our shoes.

"What kind of pudding will you make?" Huey said.

"A wonderful pudding," my father said. "It will taste like a whole raft of lemons. It will taste like a night on the sea."

Then he took down a knife and sliced five lemons in half. He squeezed the first one. Juice squirted in my eye.

"Stand back!" he said, and squeezed again. The seeds flew out on the floor. "Pick up those seeds, Huey!" he said.

Huey took the broom and swept them up.

My father cracked some eggs and put the yolks in a pan and the whites in a bowl. He rolled up his sleeves and pushed back his hair and beat up the yolks. "Sugar, Julian!" he said, and I poured in the sugar.

He went on beating. Then he put in lemon juice and cream and set the pan on the stove. The pudding bubbled and he stirred it fast. Cream splashed on the stove.

"Wipe that up, Huey!" he said.

Huey did.

It was hot by the stove. My father loosened his collar and pushed at his sleeves. The stuff in the pan was getting thicker and thicker. He held the beater up high in the air. "Just right!" he said, and sniffed in the smell of the pudding.

He whipped the egg whites and mixed them into the pudding. The pudding looked softer and lighter than air.

"Done!" he said. He washed all the pots,

splashing water on the floor, and wiped the counter so fast his hair made circles around his head.

"Perfect!" he said. "Now I'm going to take a nap. If something important happens, bother me. If nothing important happens, don't bother me. And—the pudding is for your mother. Leave the pudding alone!"

He went to the living room and was asleep in a minute, sitting straight up in his chair.

Huey and I guarded the pudding.

"Oh, it's a wonderful pudding," Huey said.

"With waves on the top like the ocean," I said.

"I wonder how it tastes," Huey said.

"Leave the pudding alone," I said.

"If I just put my finger in—there—I'll know how it tastes," Huey said.

And he did it.

"You did it!" I said. "How does it taste?"

"It tastes like a whole raft of lemons," he said. "It tastes like a night on the sea."

"You've made a hole in the pudding!" I said. "But since you did it, I'll have a taste." And it tasted like a whole night of lemons. It tasted like floating at sea.

"It's such a big pudding," Huey said. "It can't hurt to have a little more."

"Since you took more, I'll have more," I said.

"That was a bigger lick than I took!" Huey said. "I'm going to have more again."

"Whoops!" I said.

"You put in your whole hand!" Huey said. "Look at the pudding you spilled on the floor!"

"I am going to clean it up," I said. And I took the rag from the sink.

"That's not really clean," Huey said.

"It's the best I can do," I said.

"Look at the pudding!" Huey said.

It looked like craters on the moon. "We have to smooth this over," I said. "So it looks the way it did before! Let's get spoons."

And we evened the top of the pudding with spoons, and while we evened it, we ate some more.

"There isn't much left," I said.

"We were supposed to leave the pudding alone," Huey said.

"We'd better get away from here," I said. We ran into our bedroom and crawled under the bed. After a long time we heard my father's voice.

"Come into the kitchen, dear," he said. "I have something for you."

"Why, what is it?" my mother said, out in the kitchen.

Under the bed, Huey and I pressed ourselves to the wall.

"Look," said my father, out in the kitchen. "A wonderful pudding."

"Where is the pudding?" my mother said.

"WHERE ARE YOU BOYS?" my father

said. His voice went through every crack and corner of the house.

We felt like two leaves in a storm.

"WHERE ARE YOU? I SAID!" My father's voice was booming.

Huey whispered to me, "I'm scared."

We heard my father walking slowly through the rooms.

"Huey!" he called. "Julian!"

We could see his feet. He was coming into our room.

He lifted the bedspread. There was his face, and his eyes like black lightning. He grabbed us by the legs and pulled. "STAND UP!" he said.

We stood.

"What do you have to tell me?" he said.

"We went outside," Huey said, "and when we came back, the pudding was gone!"

"Then why were you hiding under the bed?" my father said.

We didn't say anything. We looked at the floor.

"I can tell you one thing," he said. "There is going to be some beating here now! There is going to be some whipping!"

The curtains at the window were shaking. Huey was holding my hand.

"Go into the kitchen!" my father said. "Right now!"

We went into the kitchen.

"Come here, Huey!" my father said.

Huey walked toward him, his hands behind his back.

"See these eggs?" my father said. He cracked them and put the yolks in a pan and set the pan on the counter. He stood a chair by the counter. "Stand up here," he said to Huey.

Huey stood on the chair by the counter.

"Now it's time for your beating!" my father said.

Huey started to cry. His tears fell in with the egg yolks.

"Take this!" my father said. My father handed him the egg beater. "Now beat those eggs," he said. "I want this to be a good beating!"

"Oh!" Huey said. He stopped crying. And he beat the egg yolks.

"Now you, Julian, stand here!" my father said.

I stood on a chair by the table.

"I hope you're ready for your whipping!"

I didn't answer. I was afraid to say yes or no.

"Here!" he said, and he set the egg whites in front of me. "I want these whipped and whipped well!"

"Yes, sir!" I said, and started whipping.

My father watched us. My mother came into the kitchen and watched us.

After a while Huey said, "This is hard work."

"That's too bad," my father said. "Your

beating's not done!" And he added sugar and cream and lemon juice to Huey's pan and put the pan on the stove. And Huey went on beating.

"My arm hurts from whipping," I said.

"That's too bad," my father said. "Your whipping's not done."

So I whipped and whipped, and Huey beat and beat.

"Hold that beater in the air, Huey!" my father said.

Huey held it in the air.

"See!" my father said. "A good pudding stays on the beater. It's thick enough now. Your beating's done." Then he turned to me. "Let's see those egg whites, Julian!" he said. They were puffed up and fluffy. "Congratulations, Julian!" he said. "Your whipping's done."

He mixed the egg whites into the pudding himself. Then he passed the pudding to my mother.

"A wonderful pudding," she said. "Would you like some, boys?"

"No thank you," we said.

She picked up a spoon. "Why, this tastes like a whole raft of lemons," she said. "This tastes like a night on the sea."

Catalog Cats

"Would you boys like to plant gardens?" my father said.

"Yes," we said.

"Good!" said my father. "I'll order a catalog."

So it was settled. But afterward, Huey said to me, "What's a catalog?"

"A catalog," I said, "is where cats come from. It's a big book full of pictures of hundreds and hundreds of cats. And when you open it up, all the cats jump out and start running around."

"I don't believe you," Huey said.

"It's true," I said.

"But why would Dad be sending for that catalog cat book?"

"The cats help with the garden," I said.

"I don't believe you," Huey said.

"It's true," I said. "You open the catalog, and the cats jump out. Then they run outside and work in the garden. White cats dig up the ground with their claws. Black cats brush the ground smooth with their tails. Yellow and brown cats roll on the seeds to push them underground so they can grow."

"I don't believe you," Huey said. "Cats don't act like that."

"Of course," I said, "*ordinary* cats don't act like that. That's why you have to get them specially—catalog cats."

"Really?" Huey said.

"Really," I said.

"I'm going to ask Dad about it," Huey said.

"You ask Dad about everything," I said. "Don't you think it's time you learned something on your own for a change?"

Huey looked hurt. "I do learn things by myself," he said. "I wonder when the catalog will come."

"Soon," I said.

The next morning Huey woke me up. "I dreamed about the catalog cats!" he said. "Only in my dream the yellow and brown ones were washing the windows and painting the house! You don't suppose they could do that, do you?"

"No, they can't do that, Huey," I said. "They don't have a way to hold rags and paintbrushes."

"I suppose not," Huey said.

Every day Huey asked my father if the catalog had come.

"Not yet," my father kept saying. He was very

pleased that Huey was so interested in the garden.

Huey dreamed about the catalog cats again. A whole team of them was carrying a giant squash to the house. One had his teeth around the stem. The others were pushing it with their shoulders and their heads.

"Do you think that's what they really do, Julian?" Huey said.

"Yes, they do that," I said.

Two weeks went by.

"Well, Huey and Julian," my father said, "today is the big day. The catalog is here."

"The catalog is here! The catalog is here! The catalog is here!" Huey said. He was dancing and twirling around.

I was thinking about going someplace else.

"What's the matter, Julian?" my father said. "Don't you want to see the catalog?"

"Oh, yes, I—want to see it," I said.

My father had the catalog under his arm. The three of us sat down on the couch.

"Open it!" Huey said.

My father opened the catalog.

Inside were bright pictures of flowers and vegetables. The catalog company would send you the seeds, and you could grow the flowers and vegetables.

Huey started turning the pages faster and faster. "Where are the cats? Where are the cats?" he kept saying.

"What cats?" my father said.

Huey started to cry.

My father looked at me. "Julian," he said, "please tell me what is going on."

"Huey thought catalogs were books with cats in them. Catalog cats," I said.

Huey sobbed. "Julian told me! Special cats — cats that work in gardens! White ones — they dig up the dirt. Black ones — they brush the ground with their tails. Yellow and brown ones — they roll on the seeds." Huey was crying harder than ever.

"Julian!" said my father.

"Yes," I said. When my father's voice gets loud, mine gets so small I can only whisper.

"Julian," my father said, "didn't you tell Huey that catalog cats are invisible?"

"No," I said.

"Julian told me they jumped out of catalogs! He said they jump out and work in gardens. As soon as you get the catalog, they go to work."

"Well," said my father, "that's very ignorant. Julian has never had a garden before in his life. I wouldn't trust a person who has never had a garden in his life to tell me about catalog cats. Would you?"

"No," Huey said slowly. He was still crying a little.

My father pulled out his handkerchief and gave it to Huey. "Now, blow your nose and listen to me," my father said.

Huey blew his nose and sat up straight on the couch. I sat back and tried to be as small as I could.

"First of all," said my father, "a lot of people have wasted a lot of time trying to see catalog

27

cats. It's a waste of time because catalog cats are the fastest animals alive. No one is as quick as a catalog cat. It may be that they really *are* visible and that they just move so quickly you can't see them. But you can feel them. When you look for a catalog cat over your right shoulder, you can feel that he is climbing the tree above your left ear. When you turn fast and look at the tree, you can feel that he has jumped out and landed behind your back. And then sometimes you feel all the little hairs on your backbone quiver—that's when you know a catalog cat is laughing at you and telling you that you are wasting your time.

"Catalog cats love gardens, and they love to work in gardens. However, they will only do

half the work. If they are in a garden where people don't do any work, the catalog cats will not do any work either. But if they are in a garden where people work hard, all the work will go twice as fast because of the catalog cats."

"When you were a boy and had a garden," Huey said, "did your garden have catalog cats?"

"Yes," my father said, "my garden had catalog cats."

"And were they your friends?" Huey said.

"Well," my father said, "they like people, but they move too fast to make friends.

"There's one more thing," my father said. "Catalog cats aren't *in* garden catalogs, and no one can order catalog cats. Catalog cats are only *around* the companies the catalogs come from. You don't order them, you request them."

"I can write up a request," I said.

"Huey can do that very well, I'm sure," my father said, "if he would like to. Would you like to, Huey?"

Huey said he would.

My father got a piece of paper and pencil.

And Huey wrote it all down:

REQUESTED:
1 dozen catalog cats
all varieties
WHOEVER
wants to come
IS WELCOME

Our Garden

We planted tomatoes, squash, onions, garlic, peas, pumpkins, and potatoes. Besides that we planted two special things we saw in the catalog, which were—

Genuine corn of the Ancients! It grows 20 feet high. Harvest your corn with a ladder. Surprise your friends and neighbors.

and

Make a house of flowers. Our beans grow ten feet tall. Grow them around string! Make a beautiful roof and walls out of their scarlet blossoms.

Huey was the one who wanted the house of flowers the most. I wanted the giant corn. My father said he wasn't sure he wanted either giant corn or a flower house, and if we wanted them, we would have to take care of them all summer by pulling weeds. We said we would.

We planted everything one Saturday. We worked all day long, getting the ground smooth and even, and laying the little seeds down in rows. The whole time I felt the catalog cats were there, swirling their tails in the air.

We finished just before the sun went down.

My mother gave Huey and me baths. She said we were darker than the garden. She said we were dirty enough that she could grow plants on our hands and knees.

When we were clean, we had supper, with chocolate pie for dessert, and went to bed.

Huey went to sleep right away. But I didn't.

I put my jacket on over my pajamas and went out the back door to the garden. In the dark it looked as if the garden was sleeping. I lay down on the grass. It was cold and a little wet.

I looked up. I thought all the catalog cats were sitting on the roof of the garage, staring at me. Over the top of the garage was the moon, a little moon with sharp horns. There were birds rustling in the dark branches of the trees.

The seeds were dreaming, I thought. I put my mouth next to the ground, and I spoke to the seeds very softly: "Grow! And you corn seeds, grow high as the house!"

In just one week the seeds did start to grow, and we watered them and weeded them. By the end of the summer we had vegetables from the

garden every night. And the corn did grow as high as the house, although there wasn't very much of it, and it was almost too tough to eat. The best thing of all was Huey's house made of flowers. After a while the flowers dropped their petals and turned into beans, and we ate the beans for supper. So what Huey made was probably the first house anyone ever played in and then ate. Catalog cats are strange—but a house you eat for dinner is stranger yet.

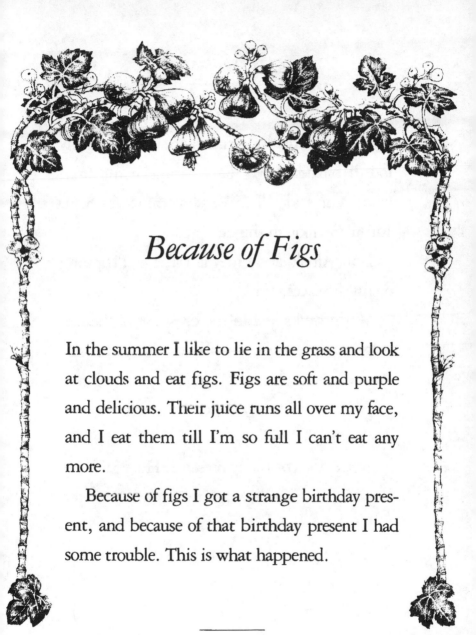

Because of Figs

In the summer I like to lie in the grass and look at clouds and eat figs. Figs are soft and purple and delicious. Their juice runs all over my face, and I eat them till I'm so full I can't eat any more.

Because of figs I got a strange birthday present, and because of that birthday present I had some trouble. This is what happened.

It all started a long time ago when I had my fourth birthday. My father came home from work and said, "I have something for you, Julian! Go look in the car."

I ran to look, and Huey ran after me, tripping on his shoelaces.

When we looked in the back seat of the car, there was a tree! A small tree with just a few leaves.

We ran back to my father. "A tree for a birth-day present!" I said.

"A tree for a birthday present!" Huey said. He was two years old, and he always repeated everything I said.

"It's a fig tree," my father told me. "It will

grow as fast as you grow, Julian, and in a few years it will have figs that you can pick and eat."

I could hardly wait to grow my own sweet juicy purple figs. We planted the tree by our back fence, and I gave it water every day. And then one morning it had two new leaves.

"Fig tree, you're growing!" I said. I thought I should be growing too. There is a mark on the wall in the bathroom of our house, where my father measures us, and I ran into the house to measure myself against my old mark. I pressed my hand against my head, flat to the wall, and checked where my hand was compared to the old mark. I wasn't any taller.

I walked outside to the fig tree. "I'm not any

taller," I said. I touched the fig tree's new leaves. "I want to grow, too!" I said. "You know how to grow, and I don't!" I told the fig tree.

The fig tree didn't say a word.

"Maybe what makes you grow will make me grow," I told it. And very quickly, I picked the fig tree's new leaves and ate them. They tasted worse than spinach. I was pretty sure they would make me grow.

I did a little growing dance around the fig tree, with my hands raised high in the air.

It worked. I stayed taller than Huey. I got taller than my fig tree. And every time my fig tree got new leaves, I saw them and ate them secretly. And when nobody was looking, I did a growing dance.

"If you don't like this, fig tree, just tell me," I'd say.

The fig tree never said a word.

After a year my father looked at my fig tree. "It's a nice little tree," he said, "but it isn't growing." And he started putting fertilizer on my tree, and he looked at it more often.

But when new leaves showed, I saw them first. And I wanted to get taller, so I ate them.

Another whole year went by.

My mark on the bathroom wall went up three inches. I was four inches taller than Huey, and my arm muscle was twice as big as his.

The fig tree hadn't grown at all.

"Fig tree," I said when I took its new leaves, "I'm sorry, but I want to grow tall."

And the fig tree didn't say a word.

One day my father was in the garden. He walked over to my fig tree. "Julian," he said, "something is the matter with your tree. It hasn't grown. It hasn't grown at all."

"Really?" I said. I didn't look at my father. I didn't look at my fig tree either.

"Do you have any idea what could be wrong?" my father asked.

I looked straight at my feet. I crossed my toes inside in my shoes. "Oh, no."

"I think that tree's just plain no good. We'll pull it out of the ground and get another one."

"Oh no! Don't do that!" I begged.

"Julian," my father said, "do you know something about this tree that I don't know?"

I didn't say anything. And I was glad, very glad, that the fig tree didn't say a word. Finally I said, "It's my tree. Give it one more chance."

"No use waiting around!" my father said. His hand was around the trunk of my tree.

"Please!" I said.

My father's hand relaxed. "After all, it *is* your tree," he said. "Just tell me when you want another one."

All afternoon I couldn't think of anything but

all the little fig leaves I'd eaten. I was pretty sure I knew why the fig tree didn't grow.

At bedtime I couldn't sleep, and when Huey went to sleep, I got up and sneaked outside to my fig tree. I told God I knew that the fig leaves belonged to the fig tree. I told the fig tree I was sorry, and I promised I would never eat its leaves again.

The fig tree didn't say a word—but the next week it got two new leaves, and kept them. That night I went to bed happy, and I dreamed a good dream. My fig tree was higher than the house, I was almost as tall as my dad, and there were big figs, juicy figs, sweet figs, falling all over the lawn.

My
Very Strange
Teeth

My mother and Huey were listening. My father and I were talking.

"Well," my father said, "if you wait long enough, it will fall out." He was talking about my tooth, my right bottom front tooth.

"How long do I have to wait?" I asked.

Because I had *two* right bottom front teeth—one firm little new one pushing in, and one wiggly old one.

"I can't say," my father said. "Maybe a month, maybe two months. Maybe less."

"I don't want to wait," I said. "I want *one* tooth there, and I don't want to wait two months!"

"All right!" said my father. "I'll take care of it!" He jumped out of his chair and ran out the door to the garage. He was back in a minute, carrying something—a pair of pliers!

"Your tooth is a little loose already," my father said. "So I'll just put the pliers in your mouth for a second, twist, and the tooth will come out. You won't feel a thing!"

"I won't feel a thing?" I looked at the pliers—huge, black-handled pliers with a long pointed tip. I thought I *would* feel a thing. I thought it would hurt.

"Shall I?" said my dad. He raised the pliers toward my mouth.

"NO!" I said. "Not that way! Don't you know any other way to take out a tooth?"

"Well," he answered, "when I was a boy the main way was with a pair of pliers—but there was another way. Just you wait."

He jumped up again and ran to the closet. When he came back, he had a spool of black thread. Thread didn't look as painful as pliers.

"This is a simple way," my father said. "Just

let me tie this thread around your old tooth."

"All right," I said.

Very carefully my father tied the end of the thread around my old tooth. That didn't hurt.

"Now," my father said, "stand here by the door."

I stood by the kitchen door, and my father tied the other end of the thread to the doorknob.

"Now what?" I said.

"Now," my father said, "you just close your eyes . . ."

"What are you going to do?" I asked. I wasn't going to close my eyes when I didn't know what was happening.

"This is a *good* method from the old days," my

father said. "You close your eyes. Then—very suddenly—I shove the kitchen door shut. Snap! The thread pulls the tooth right out!"

I looked at the kitchen door. It was a lot bigger than I was—and about 20 million times bigger than my tooth.

"Won't it—hurt?" I was really afraid I might lose my whole head with the tooth.

"Oh, just a little," my father said. "Just for a *second*."

"No thanks," I said. "Please take this thread off my tooth!"

"All right then." My father shrugged his shoulders and took the string off my tooth.

"Don't you know *any other* way?"

"There is one other way," my father said. "Go into the bathroom, stand over the sink, and just keep pushing the tooth with your finger till it comes out."

"Will that hurt?"

"You can stop pushing when it hurts," my father said. "Of course it takes longer—I would be very glad to do it with either the pliers or the doorknob."

"No thanks," I said. I started pushing on my tooth with my finger. "Why can't I push it out here?" I asked. "Why do I have to do it over the sink?"

"When you get the tooth out," my father said, "it'll bleed. That's why you take the tooth out over the sink—so you have cold water to rinse your mouth and stop the bleeding."

"*How much* bleeding?"

"Some. Enough so you should use the sink."

I decided right then that my old tooth could stay in my mouth right beside the new one as long as it wanted —two months, two years, any time.

"I've changed my mind," I said. "That tooth can stay, even if it is stupid to have two teeth where one should be."

"It's not stupid," my mother said, "just unusual. You have very special teeth. I bet prehistoric cavemen would have liked to have your teeth."

"Why?"

"They ate a lot of raw meat," my mother said. "It must have been hard for a cave boy to eat raw meat with teeth missing. But you have two teeth in the space of one. You could have eaten mastodon meat or saber-toothed tiger meat, or anything the hunters brought home."

A cave boy with two teeth in place of one. I wished I had a time machine to go back to the *very* old days—before pliers and before doorknobs —back to the caves. I curled my lower lip under.

"You look like a cave boy," my mother said.

"You should show the kids at school your teeth," Huey said.

"Maybe I will," I said.

I went to my room and made a sign for myself. It read—

See Cave-Boy Teeth
one cent
1¢   1¢

I wore the sign at recess the next day.

My friends came around. "What does *that* mean?" they asked.

"Uh. Uh." I grunted and held up a penny. I couldn't explain. If I talked, they'd see my teeth for free.

After a while one girl gave me a penny, and I showed her my special cave-boy teeth. Some of the other kids had missing teeth, but nobody had two teeth in one space like mine.

I ran all the way home after school to tell my mother what happened. I said, "Tomorrow I'll show more kids!"

I picked up an apple that lay on the kitchen table and took a big bite.

"Ow!" I said, because I could feel my old tooth twist in my mouth. In a minute, without too much blood, it was lying on my hand. "OW!" I said again, not because it hurt, but because right then was the end of my special, mastodon-eating, double-biting, cave-boy teeth.

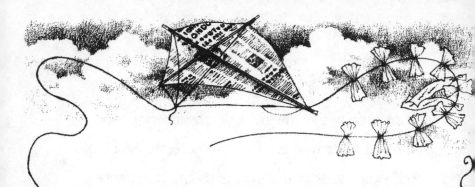

Gloria
Who Might Be
My Best Friend

If you have a girl for a friend, people find out and tease you. That's why I didn't want a girl for a friend—not until this summer, when I met Gloria.

It happened one afternoon when I was walking down the street by myself. My mother was visiting a friend of hers, and Huey was visiting a friend of his. Huey's friend is five and so I think he is too young to play with. And there aren't any kids just my age. I was walking down the street feeling lonely.

A block from our house I saw a moving van in front of a brown house, and men were carrying in chairs and tables and bookcases and boxes full of I don't know what. I watched for a while, and suddenly I heard a voice right behind me.

"Who are you?"

I turned around and there was a girl in a yellow dress. She looked the same age as me.

She had curly hair that was braided into two pigtails with red ribbons at the ends.

"I'm Julian," I said. "Who are you?"

"I'm Gloria," she said. "I come from Newport. Do you know where Newport is?"

I wasn't sure, but I didn't tell Gloria. "It's a town on the ocean," I said.

"Right," Gloria said. "Can you turn a cartwheel?"

She turned sideways herself and did two cartwheels on the grass.

I had never tried a cartwheel before, but I tried to copy Gloria. My hands went down in the grass, my feet went up in the air, and—I fell over.

I looked at Gloria to see if she was laughing at

me. If she was laughing at me, I was going to go home and forget about her.

But she just looked at me very seriously and said, "It takes practice," and then I liked her.

"I know where there's a bird's nest in your yard," I said.

"Really?" Gloria said. "There weren't any trees in the yard, or any birds, where I lived before."

I showed her where a robin lives and has eggs. Gloria stood up on a branch and looked in. The eggs were small and pale blue. The mother robin squawked at us, and she and the father robin flew around our heads.

"They want us to go away," Gloria said. She

got down from the branch, and we went around to the front of the house and watched the moving men carry two rugs and a mirror inside.

"Would you like to come over to my house?" I said.

"All right," Gloria said, "if it is all right with my mother." She ran in the house and asked.

It was all right, so Gloria and I went to my house, and I showed her my room and my games and my rock collection, and then I made strawberry Kool-Aid and we sat at the kitchen table and drank it.

"You have a red mustache on your mouth," Gloria said.

"You have a red mustache on your mouth, too," I said.

Gloria giggled, and we licked off the mustaches with our tongues.

"I wish you'd live here a long time," I told Gloria.

Gloria said, "I wish I would too.

"I know the best way to make wishes," Gloria said.

"What's that?" I asked.

"First you make a kite. Do you know how to make one?"

"Yes," I said, "I know how." I know how to make good kites because my father taught me.

We make them out of two crossed sticks and folded newspaper.

"All right," Gloria said, "that's the first part of making wishes that come true. So let's make a kite."

We went out into the garage and spread out sticks and newspaper and made a kite. I fastened on the kite string and went to the closet and got rags for the tail.

"Do you have some paper and two pencils?" Gloria asked. "Because now we make the wishes."

I didn't know what she was planning, but I went in the house and got pencils and paper.

"All right," Gloria said. "Every wish you

want to have come true you write on a long thin piece of paper. You don't tell me your wishes, and I don't tell you mine. If you tell, your wishes don't come true. Also, if you look at the other person's wishes, your wishes don't come true."

Gloria sat down on the garage floor and started writing her wishes. I wanted to see what they were—but I went to the other side of the garage and wrote my own wishes instead. I wrote:

1. I wish I could see the catalog cats.
2. I wish the fig tree would be the tallest in town.
3. I wish I'd be a great soccer player.
4. I wish I could ride in an airplane.
5. I wish Gloria would stay here and be my best friend.

I folded my five wishes in my fist and went over to Gloria.

"How many wishes did you make?" Gloria asked.

"Five," I said. "How many did you make?"

"Two," Gloria said.

I wondered what they were.

"Now we put the wishes on the tail of the kite," Gloria said. "Every time we tie one piece of rag on the tail, we fasten a wish in the knot. You can put yours in first."

I fastened mine in, and then Gloria fastened in hers, and we carried the kite into the yard.

"You hold the tail," I told Gloria, "and I'll pull."

We ran through the back yard with the kite, passed the garden and the fig tree, and went into the open field beyond our yard.

The kite started to rise. The tail jerked heavily like a long white snake. In a minute the kite passed the roof of my house and was climbing toward the sun.

We stood in the open field, looking up at it. I was wishing I would get my wishes.

"I know it's going to work!" Gloria said.

"How do you know?"

"When we take the kite down," Gloria told me, "there shouldn't be one wish in the tail. When the wind takes all your wishes, that's when you know it's going to work."

The kite stayed up for a long time. We both held the string. The kite looked like a tiny black spot in the sun, and my neck got stiff from looking at it.

"Shall we pull it in?" I asked.

"All right," Gloria said.

We drew the string in more and more until, like a tired bird, the kite fell at our feet.

We looked at the tail. All our wishes were gone. Probably they were still flying higher and higher in the wind.

Maybe I would see the catalog cats and get to be a good soccer player and have a ride in an airplane and the tallest fig tree in town. And Gloria would be my best friend.

"Gloria," I said, "did you wish we would be friends?"

"You're not supposed to ask me that!" Gloria said.

"I'm sorry," I answered. But inside I was smiling. I guessed one thing Gloria wished for. I was pretty sure we would be friends.

ABOUT THE AUTHOR

Ann Cameron is the bestselling author of the Julian's World series and many other popular books for children. She lives in Guatemala. Find her online at anncameronbooks.com.

Once there was a day so hot
that even frogs wore shoes!
Julian has SO many more stories to tell!

Read on for a peek at
Julian's next adventure!

Excerpt text copyright © 1986 by Ann Cameron. Excerpt illustrations copyright © 1986 by Ann Strugnell. Published in the United States by Random House Children's Books, a division of Penguin Random House LLC, New York. Originally published in hardcover by Alfred A. Knopf, an imprint of Random House Children's Books, a division of Penguin Random House LLC, New York, in 1986.

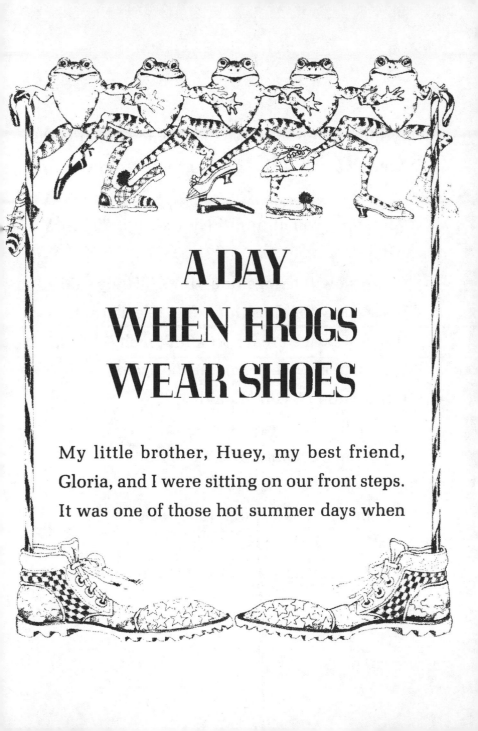

A DAY
WHEN FROGS
WEAR SHOES

My little brother, Huey, my best friend,
Gloria, and I were sitting on our front steps.
It was one of those hot summer days when

everything stands still. We didn't know what to do. We were watching the grass grow. It didn't grow fast.

"You know something?" Gloria said. "This is a slow day."

"It's so slow the dogs don't bark," Huey said.

"It's so slow the flies don't fly," Gloria said.

"It's so slow ice cream wouldn't melt," I said.

"If we had any ice cream," Huey said.

"But we don't," Gloria said.

We watched the grass some more.

"We better do something," I said.

"Like what?" Gloria asked.

"We could go visit Dad," Huey said.

"That's a terrible idea," I said.

"Why?" Huey asked. "I like visiting Dad."

My father has a shop about a mile from our house, where he fixes cars. Usually it is fun to visit him. If he has customers, he always introduces us as if we were important guests. If he doesn't have company, sometimes he lets us ride in the cars he puts up on the lift. Sometimes he buys us treats.

"Huey," I said, "usually, visiting Dad is a good idea. Today, it's a dangerous idea."

"Why?" Gloria said.

"Because we're bored," I said. "My dad hates it when people are bored. He says the world is so interesting nobody should ever be bored."

"I see," Gloria said, as if she didn't.

"So we'll go see him," Huey said, "and we just won't tell him we're bored. We're bored, but we won't tell him."

"Just so you remember that!" I said.

"Oh, I'll remember," Huey said.

Huey was wearing his angel look. When he has that look, you know he'll never remember anything.

Huey and I put on sweat bands. Gloria put on dark glasses. We started out.

The sun shined up at us from the sidewalks. Even the shadows on the street were hot as blankets.

Huey picked up a stick and scratched it along the sidewalk. "Oh, we're bored," he muttered. "Bored, bored, bored, bored, bored!"

"Huey!" I yelled. I wasn't bored anymore. I was nervous.

Finally we reached a sign:

RALPH'S CAR HOSPITAL
Punctures
Rust
Dents & Bashes
Bad Brakes
Bad Breaks
Unusual Complaints

That's my dad's sign. My dad is Ralph.

The parking lot had three cars in it. Dad was inside the shop, lifting the hood of another car. He didn't have any customers with him, so we didn't get to shake hands and feel like visiting mayors or congressmen.

"Hi, Dad," I said.

"Hi!" my dad said.

"We're—" Huey said.

I didn't trust Huey. I stepped on his foot.

"We're on a hike," I said.

"Well, nice of you to stop by," my father said. "If you want, you can stay awhile and help me."

"O.K.," we said.

So Huey sorted nuts and bolts. Gloria shined fenders with a rag. I held a new windshield wiper while my dad put it on a car window.

"Nice work, Huey and Julian and Gloria!" my dad said when we were done.

And then he sent us to the store across the street to buy paper cups and ice cubes and a can of frozen lemonade.

We mixed the lemonade in the shop. Then we sat out under the one tree by the side of the driveway and drank all of it.

"Good lemonade!" my father said. "So what are you kids going to do now?"

"Oh, hike!" I said.

"You know," my father answered, "I'm surprised at you kids picking a hot day like today for a hike. The ground is so hot. On a day like this, frogs wear shoes!"

"They do?" Huey said.

"Especially if they go hiking," my father said. "Of course, a lot of frogs, on a day like this, would stay home. So I wonder why you kids are hiking."

Sometimes my father notices too much. Then he gets yellow lights shining in his eyes, asking you to tell the whole truth. That's when I know to look at my feet.

"Oh," I said, "we *like* hiking."

But Gloria didn't know any better. She looked into my father's eyes. "Really," she said, "this wasn't a real hike. We came to see you."

"Oh, I see!" my father said, looking pleased.

"Because we were bored," Huey said.

My father jumped up so fast he tipped over his lemonade cup. "BORED!" my father yelled. "You were BORED?"

He picked up his cup and waved it in the air.

"And you think *I* don't get BORED?" my father roared, sprinkling out a few last drops of lemonade from his cup. "You think I don't get bored fixing cars when it's hot enough that frogs wear shoes?"

HAVE YOU READ ALL THE BOOKS IN THE

A TO Z Mysteries®

SERIES?

Help Dink, Josh, and Ruth Rose . . .

. . . solve
mysteries
from A to Z!

MOST VALUABLE PLAYERS
MVP

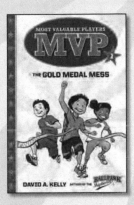

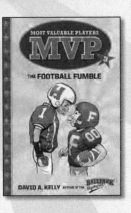

★
**Always
show spirit!**
★
**Bring their
all to any
sport!**
★
**Never
give up!**
★

**A NEW SERIES
FROM THE
AUTHOR OF THE**

1256

RANDOMHOUSEKIDS.COM RHCB

New friends. New adventures.
Find a new series... just for you!

ISADORA MOON

Isadora Moon Goes to School

For ballerina and fairy and vampire lovers

COMMANDER IN CHEESE

Commander in Cheese: The Big Move

For adventurers

JULIAN'S WORLD: THE STORIES JULIAN TELLS

Julian's World: The Stories Julian Tells
Ann Cameron

For storytellers

PUPPY PIRATES

Puppy Pirates: Stowaway!

For dog lovers

PURRMAIDS

Purrmaids: The Scaredy Cat

For mermaid and cat lovers

BALLPARK Mysteries

Ballpark Mysteries Super Special #1: The World Series Curse

For sports fans

Isadora Moon: Cover art © by Harriet Muncaster. Commander in Cheese: Cover art © by AG Ford. Julian's World: Cover art © by Luz Tapia. Puppy Pirates: Cover art © by Robert Papp. Puppy Pirates: Cover art © by Andrew Farley. Ballpark Mysteries: Cover art © by Mark Meyers.

RHCB **RHCBooks.com**